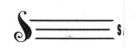

THE TIME MACHINE

H. G. WELLS

ADAPTED BY

Emily Hutchinson

SADDLEBACK PUBLISHING, INC.

SADDLEBACK *Classics*

The Adventures of Tom Sawyer
Dr. Jekyll and Mr. Hyde
Dracula
Great Expectations
Jane Eyre
Moby Dick
Robinson Crusoe
The Time Machine

Development and Production: Laurel Associates, Inc.
Cover and Interior Art: Black Eagle Productions

SADDLEBACK PUBLISHING, INC.
3505 Cadillac Ave., Building F-9
Costa Mesa, CA 92626-1443

ISBN 1-56254-279-6

Printed in the United States of America
05 04 03   9 8 7 6 5 4 3 2 1

CONTENTS

1 We See the Time Machine

The Time Traveler, as we shall call him, was speaking to us of deep matters. His gray eyes were shining, and his usually pale face was bright. We had just finished dinner at his house that night in 1895. There were six of us there—a doctor, a very young man, a mayor, a psychologist, a storekeeper named Filby, and me. All of us admired our host for his bright mind and his many inventions. In fact, we were sitting in comfortable chairs that he had invented. As he spoke, he pointed at us excitedly.

"You must follow me carefully," he said. "Most of the math that they taught you at school is based on incorrect ideas."

"Ha! Do you expect us to believe that?" said Filby. He was a man who liked to argue.

"I can prove it. They taught you that all

things have shape and form, right? We measure things by how long, high, and wide they are. These are the three dimensions of space, aren't they?"

"Correct," said the mayor.

"Well, what about time? Clearly, any real body must also exist in time. That is the *fourth* way to measure things."

"What? I don't follow you," said Filby.

"Let me explain," said the Time Traveler. "For anything to be real to us, it must last long enough for us to know that it's there. So there are really four dimensions. There's only one difference between time and space. The difference is that our consciousness moves along time in just one direction— from the beginning to the end of our lives.

"Think about this: Here is a portrait of a man at 8 years old, another at 15, another at 17, another at 23, and so on. All of these are three-dimensional pictures of a four-dimensional being. In other words, this is still the same person, even though the pictures show the man's different ages through time. Some scientists are now telling us that time is only a kind of space."

"Wait!" said the doctor. "That doesn't make sense. If time is really just a fourth dimension of space, why can't we move freely through it, as we do in space?"

The Time Traveler smiled. "Are you *sure* we can move freely in space? We can go right and left, and backward and forward. I admit that we can move freely in two dimensions. But how about up and down? Gravity limits us there."

"Not exactly," said the doctor. "There are balloons."

"But before balloons, except for jumping, we could not move up and down."

"Still, we could move a little way up and down," said the doctor.

"Easier, *far* easier, down than up."

"Well, we cannot move at all in time. None of us can get away from the present moment," said the doctor.

"My dear sir, that is just where you are wrong. We are always getting away from the present moment. We travel at the same speed from the cradle to the grave. It is just as we would travel *down* if we began our lives 50 miles above the earth."

The psychologist then spoke up. "There is something wrong with your ideas. We *can* move about in all directions of space, but we cannot move about in time."

"That is my great discovery, the reason I have invited you here tonight. You are wrong to say we cannot move about in time. For instance, if I remember something very clearly, I go back to the time it happened. I become absentminded, as you say. I jump back for a moment. Of course, we cannot *stay* back for any length of time, any more than we can stay six feet above the ground. But we can go up against gravity in a balloon. Why should we not hope to stop or speed up our travel through time? And why not even turn around and travel the other way?"

"Oh, that is ridiculous!" cried Filby.

"Why do you say that?" asked our host.

"Huh! I suppose you can show black is white by argument," said Filby, "but you will never convince *me*!"

"What if I showed you proof?" asked the

Time Traveler with a twinkle in his eye.

"It would be wonderful for history teachers," said the psychologist. "They could travel back in time and see for themselves what really happened."

"Then there is the *future*," said the very young man. "You could invest your money, let it grow with interest, and hurry on ahead. By the time you got there, you'd be rich!"

"But where is your proof?" asked the psychologist.

The Time Traveler smiled at us. Then he walked slowly out of the room. We heard him walking down the long hall to his lab. While he was gone, Filby started talking about a magic show he had once seen. Before he finished, however, the Time Traveler had returned.

The thing he held in his hand was a shining metal form. It was about the size of a small clock, and very delicate. Some parts of it looked like glass.

He set it on a table in front of the fire. Then he drew up a chair and sat down. We were all looking at the model very closely.

Even now it seems impossible that any kind of trick could have been played on us under these conditions.

"This is only a model," said the Time Traveler. "It is my plan for a machine to travel through time."

The doctor looked closely at the thing. "It's beautifully made," he said grudgingly.

"It took two years to make," said the Time Traveler. He pointed to a seat on the machine. "This is where the time traveler will sit. When I press this white bar forward, the machine will go into the future. The other bar will send it into the past. When I press down on the white bar, it will be gone forever. That's because there is no one on it to bring it back. Have a good look at it. Look at the table, too, and be sure that I am playing no trick. I don't want any of you to say that I fooled you."

We were all quiet for a moment. Then the Time Traveler reached toward the bar. "No," he said suddenly. "Give me your hand." He took the psychologist's hand in his own and had him press the bar. So it was the psychologist himself who sent the model on its voyage. The machine began to glow. There was a breath of wind, and the lamp flame jumped. One of the candles on the mantel was blown out. The little machine glittered for a moment. Then it seemed as if we could see through it. Suddenly it was gone—vanished! Except for the lamp, the table was bare.

Everyone in the room was silent for a minute. "Well?" asked the Time Traveler.

"Do you mean to say that the machine has traveled in time?" asked the doctor.

"Yes," said the Time Traveler. "What is more, I have a big machine nearly finished. When it is put together, I plan to have a journey of my own."

"Do you really think that machine has gone into the future?" said Filby.

"Into the future or the past. I don't know which for certain. Would you like to see the Time Machine itself?" asked the Time Traveler. Without waiting for an answer, he took up the lamp and led us to his lab.

There we saw a larger model of the one that

had disappeared. But this one wasn't finished.

"Look here," said the doctor. "Are you really serious? Or is this a trick—like that ghost you showed us last Christmas?"

"I plan to explore time on that machine," said the Time Traveler. "Isn't that plain? I've never been more serious in my life."

None of us knew quite how to take it.

I caught Filby's eye over the doctor's shoulder. He gave me a wink!

§2 One Week Later

I don't think any of us really believed in the Time Machine. The fact is, the Time Traveler was one of those men who are too clever to be believed. You never knew when he was joking. If Filby had told us the same story, we would have been more likely to believe him. That's because Filby is not clever enough to make up a story like that.

The next Thursday, I was invited to dinner again at the Time Traveler's house. When I got there, four or five men were already waiting. The doctor said, "It's 7:30 now. I suppose we'd better have dinner."

"Where's our host?" I asked.

"Well, it's rather odd," said the doctor. "He left this note. He says he may be late. If he's not here by 7:00, we're to start dinner without him. He says that he'll explain everything to us when he gets here."

So we sat down and rang for the servants. The psychologist, the doctor, and I were the only ones who had been here last week. The other guests were an editor, a reporter, and a shy man who didn't speak all evening. As we talked about where our host might be, we heard the door from the hall open slowly and quietly.

Since I was facing the door, I saw him first. "Hello!" I said. "At last!" The Time Traveler stood before us. I gave a cry of surprise as I took a closer look at him.

"Good heavens, man! What's the matter?" cried the doctor, who saw him next. Then all the others turned toward the door.

He looked terrible. His coat was dusty and dirty. The sleeves were smeared with something green and oily. His hair was a mess, and it now seemed grayer. His face was pale. His chin had a half-healed cut on it. He looked tired and weak. For a moment he stood in the doorway, as if dazzled by the light. Then he slowly came into the room. He walked with a limp. We stared at him in silence, expecting him to say something.

He said not a word, but came directly to the table and pointed to the wine bottle. The editor filled a glass and gave it to him. He drank it and gave us a weak smile.

"What on earth have you been up to, man?" the doctor asked. The Time Traveler did not seem to hear him.

"Don't let me disturb you. I'm all right." He held out his glass for more wine, and drank it at once. "That's good," he said. His eyes grew brighter, and a faint color came into his face.

He looked around the warm, comfortable room. Then he spoke again. "I'm going to wash and dress now. Then I'll come down and explain things. Be sure to save me some of that roast. I'm starving for a bit of meat."

As he walked away, I noticed why he was limping. He had nothing on his feet but a pair of torn, blood-stained socks. For a moment I thought about following him to his room. But then I remembered how he hated any fuss about himself.

I heard the editor say, *Strange Behavior*

15

Noted in Famous Scientist. He always enjoyed speaking in headlines.

I said that it had something to do with a time machine, but no one believed me. The editor asked, as if it were a joke, "Don't they have any clothes brushes in the future?" All through the meal, the men made jokes. They were still laughing when the Time Traveler came back to the table.

"Where's my plate?" he asked. "What a treat it is to stick a fork into meat again! I won't say another word until I get some food into my system. Thanks for your patience. Now please pass the salt."

"Just one question," I said. "Have you been time traveling?"

"Yes," said the Time Traveler. Then he started eating. At last the Time Traveler pushed his plate away and looked at us. "I suppose I must apologize," he said. "I was simply *starving*! I've had a most amazing time, and I'll tell you all about it. But first come into the other room. It's too long a story to tell over dirty plates." Then he led the way to the next room. It was the same room in which we had first seen the model of the Time Machine.

After we had all sat down, he said, "If you like, I will tell you the story of what has happened to me. But you must not interrupt me. Most of it may sound like lying. Well, so be it! It's true—every word of it—all the same.

"I was in my lab at 4:00 this afternoon. Since then, I've lived eight days . . . such days as no human being ever lived before! I'm nearly worn out, but I'll tell you this story before I go to bed. But no interruptions! Is it agreed?"

"Agreed," said the editor. When the rest of us quickly agreed as well, the Time Traveler began to tell his amazing story.

3 Traveling Through Time

"I told some of you last Thursday about how the Time Machine worked. I even showed you the machine itself in my lab. There it is now. But it is worn from travel. One of the control bars is cracked. The other bar is bent, but luckily it still works.

"I thought I'd have it all ready last Friday—the day after we had dinner. But at the last minute, I found that one of the bars was too short. I didn't get the machine working properly until today.

"At 10:00 this morning, I made some last-minute checks. I put one more drop of oil on the quartz rod, and then I sat in the saddle. I took the control bars in my hands and pushed the forward bar.

"Right away, I became dizzy. I felt as if I were falling. I pressed the other bar to stop the machine. Then I looked around and saw the lab was exactly as it had been when I came in. Had anything happened? I looked at the clock. When I began, it was 10:00. Now it was 3:30 in the afternoon!

"I took a deep breath, pushed the forward bar again, and went off with a thud. The lab got hazy and went dark. My housekeeper came into the lab and walked toward the garden door. She didn't seem to see me. I imagine it took her a minute or two to cross the room. But to me it looked as if she shot across the room like a rocket!

"I pressed the bar forward even more. Night came, then day, then night again, faster and faster. Suddenly I couldn't see my lab at all. A buzzing sound filled my ears.

"I am afraid I cannot tell you *exactly* how time traveling feels, but it is very unpleasant. You have the feeling that you are going too fast. You think that if you hit something, you'll die from the crash. I saw the sun hopping across the sky, each minute marking a day. As I traveled even faster, night and day became one constant grayness. I saw all the phases of the moon in the blink of an eye.

"I saw buildings rise and fall in minutes. Soon I noticed that I was traveling at over a year a minute. I could see white snow followed by the bright green of spring.

"At first I didn't think of stopping. But soon I wondered about what I would find. What wonderful things would I see? When I pulled back on the bar, the Time Machine tipped over. I was flung through the air.

"I heard a sound like a clap of thunder. Then I think I passed out for a few minutes. When I came to, I looked around me. I was on a little green lawn, surrounded by flowers. I noticed that their blossoms were dropping under the beating of hail. In a moment, I was wet to the skin. I remember thinking, 'This is a fine welcome for a man who has traveled so many years to see you.'

"I stood up and looked for a place to get out of the hailstorm. Beyond the flowers, I saw a huge figure carved out of white marble. It looked something like a sphinx with wings. Because the wings were spread out, the statue seemed to hover in the air. I saw that the base was made of bronze, which was green with age. Its face was turned toward me. There was a faint smile on its lips. The statue was weather worn. I had the feeling it had become rotten from inside— not from age, but from sickness.

"I began to think about the world I had come to. How might people have changed? What if they were very cruel? To them, I might seem like some old-world, savage animal. They might think I was so dangerous they would kill me!

"As the skies cleared, I saw other vast shapes. They were huge white buildings. Suddenly I became afraid. I turned to the Time Machine and tried to pull it upright. I felt perhaps as a bird may feel, knowing that the hawk flies above and will soon swoop down. My fear rapidly grew worse. I struggled with the machine and finally got it back up. With one hand planted on the seat, I got ready to mount again.

"But now that I knew I could leave at any time, my courage returned. I looked back at the big white buildings. In an opening high up in the wall of the closest house, I saw a group of figures dressed in rich soft robes. It was clear that they had seen me.

"Then I heard voices. Some men were running toward me. One of these came up to where I stood with my machine. He was a slight figure—perhaps four feet tall. He was dressed in a short purple robe, tied at the waist with a leather belt. He wore sandals on his feet. His legs were bare and so was his head. It was then I noticed for the first time how very warm the air was.

"The man struck me as being quite beautiful and graceful. But I also got the impression that he was very weak. At the sight of him, I got my confidence back. I took my hand from the machine."

4 The People of the Future

"In another moment, the man and I were standing face to face. He came up to me, looked into my eyes, and laughed. He showed no fear. Then he turned to two others who were with him. He spoke to them in a strange but very sweet-sounding language.

"Others were coming, and soon eight or ten of these little people were all around me. One of them spoke to me. I shook my head and pointed to my ears. I was trying to tell them that I didn't understand their language. One of them stepped forward and then touched my hand. Then several others also touched me—on my back and shoulders. They wanted to make sure I was real.

"I was not a bit afraid. After all, I thought I could pick up a dozen of them at once and fling them away. But then I also saw them trying to touch the Time Machine. Quickly, I went to it and took off the little bars that would set it in motion. I put them in my pocket for safekeeping. Then I turned back to the little people. I was determined to get through to them somehow.

"I looked more closely at these strange creatures. Their faces looked like those of little dolls. Their hair was curly and ended sharply at the neck and cheek. There was not the slightest suggestion of hair on their faces. Their ears were small, and so were their mouths. They had bright red, rather thin lips. Their little chins came to a point. The eyes were large and mild.

"What was surprising was the way they acted toward me. The dials on the Time Machine told me that I was in the year 802,701. I had always thought that the people of the future would be ahead of us in knowledge, art—everything. Then one of them asked me a question that even a five-year-old of 1895 wouldn't ask. With hand gestures, he wanted to know if I had come from the sun, in a thunderstorm!

"I knew I could never explain the truth to them. So I just nodded my head. I pointed to the sun, and made the sound of thunder.

"They all took a few steps back and bowed. Then one came laughing toward me, carrying a chain of beautiful flowers. He put it around my neck. Soon they were all running back and forth flinging flowers upon me. In another minute I was almost covered with flowers!

"One of them took me by the hand and led me to the nearest building. As we walked by the huge marble sphinx, it seemed to smile at me. I smiled, too, for the whole thing seemed like a big joke. So *this* was the world of the future? Its people were no smarter than five-year-olds!

"The building had a huge entry. In fact, everything about it was large. For the moment, I forgot that the Time Machine was left deserted among the flowers.

"The arch of the doorway was richly carved. But I saw that the decorations were very badly broken. As we walked into the great hall, I could see that nobody took care of it either. The floor was made of very hard white metal. But as hard as the metal was, it, too, showed signs of wear. It looked as if thousands of little feet had worn it away over thousands of years.

"The hall was full of tables made of polished stone. These were raised about a foot from the floor. Upon these tables were heaps of fruit. I recognized some raspberries and oranges, but for the most part the fruits were unfamiliar to me.

"Between the tables were many cushions.

The little people sat on them, signaling for me to do the same. They began to eat the fruit with their hands. They threw the peels into round openings built in the sides of the tables. I followed their example, for I felt thirsty and hungry.

"I looked around the hall. The stained-glass windows were broken in many places. The curtains that hung across the lower end were thick with dust. And the corner of the marble table near me was cracked. Still, the general effect was quite rich. A few hundred people were dining in the hall. Most of them were watching me as they ate. All wore the same soft, yet strong, silky material.

"Fruit, by the way, was all they ate. Indeed, I found out later that horses, cattle, pigs, sheep, and dogs had long ago become extinct. But the fruits were very good.

"As soon as I had eaten enough, I decided to start learning the language of these people. I pointed to one piece of fruit and started making sounds. I made my voice go up, to mean that I was asking a question. They thought it was funny. But I kept at it, and soon I learned the names of about 10 fruits and even their verb, meaning 'to eat.'

"I soon discovered a very strange thing about my little hosts. That was their lack of ongoing interest. I was something new to them. They would come up to me, just to get a good look. Then, like easily bored children, they would soon wander away after some other toy. Nothing seemed to hold their attention for very long.

"It was evening when I left the great hall. Suddenly, I was surprised at how different everything looked. When I left my house in 1895, I was in the heart of London. The river was not far from my home.

"Now I went to a hilltop, about a mile and a half away. I looked around. There was no sign of the city. I could see that even the river had changed over the years. It was about a mile away from where it used to be!

"I walked back toward the great hall. Soon I came across the ruins of a big building. Now it was just a crumbled heap of trash. Thick plants were growing in the broken blocks of stone. Later, I would have a very strange experience here. But I will speak of that in its proper place in my story.

"Looking around, I saw palace-like buildings here and there among the hills. I realized that there were no small houses. I saw then that the idea of the single house—even the private household—had vanished. The little people all lived together in the huge buildings. They ate together, and they all wore the same kind of clothes.

"Suddenly I had another thought. Even the *people* of the future all looked very much alike. There was not much difference in the appearance of men and women. That made sense, of course. In this land of the future, violence was rare, and the children were all safe. So there was no real need for a strong male to protect them. This, I must remind you, was my thought at the time. Later, I would find out how wrong I was."

The Time Machine Disappears

"As I stood thinking, the full moon came up. I shivered with the cold of the night. I knew I had to find a place to sleep.

"I looked for the building I knew. Then I saw the sphinx. It got clearer as the rising moon grew brighter. I looked at the lawn again. I could see the flowering bushes. But suddenly a chill came over me. 'No,' I said to myself. 'That can't be the lawn.'

"But it *was* the lawn, for the white face of the sphinx was facing it. Suddenly I was gripped by fear. My wonderful Time Machine was gone!

"I thought of losing my own time, of being left helpless in this strange new world. I could feel the fear in my throat, stopping my breathing. I ran down the hill. I must have covered two miles in ten minutes or so. And as you know, I am not a young man.

"When I reached the lawn, the Time Machine was nowhere in sight. Above me was the sphinx, on its bronze base. Now it seemed to smile, as if mocking me.

"I knew that the little people were not strong enough or smart enough to move my machine. This led me to believe that some other power was at work here. I had the only levers that could make the machine move in time, so I knew it must be here somewhere. But where could it be hidden?

"Like a crazy man, I searched through the bushes all around the sphinx. I remember that I scared some white animal. In the dim light, I took it to be a small deer. Only later did I learn just what that animal was.

"I ran back to the big hall. The full moon lit my way. The big hall was dark and empty. I lit a match and hurried past the dusty curtains, of which I have already told you.

"There I found a second great hall covered with cushions. About 20 of the little people were sleeping there. 'Where is my Time Machine?' I yelled. By then I was crying like an angry child, shaking them awake. Some of the little people laughed, but most of them looked very frightened.

"Suddenly, I couldn't bear to look at them. I ran back outside, under the moonlight. I heard cries of terror. Their little feet were running this way and that. I do not remember all I did as the moon crossed the sky. I felt like a strange animal in an unknown world. My memory is of being very tired and miserable. At last, I lay on the ground near the sphinx. I slept, and when I woke again it was full day.

"I sat up and tried to remember how I had got there. Then things became clear in my mind. I thought hard about my situation. 'Suppose the worst,' I said to myself. 'Suppose the machine is lost forever. I must be calm and learn the way of these people. I must find out how to get materials and tools. In the end, perhaps, I may make another Time Machine.' That would be my only hope.

"I thought that probably the machine had only been taken away. I must find its hiding place, and get it back. With that thought in mind, I began to look closely at the ground near where the Time Machine had been. I found some strange narrow footprints—like those made by a sloth or a similar animal— near the sphinx.

"I looked more closely at the base of the sphinx. It was made of bronze panels. I rapped at it and discovered that it was hollow. There were no handles or keyholes. I figured that the panels, if they were doors, opened from the inside. It took no great mental effort to figure out that my Time Machine was inside the base of the sphinx. But how it got there was a different problem.

"Maybe the little people knew. I saw two of them coming through the bushes. I stopped them and led them toward the sphinx. But they got scared and ran off. I was used to the little people not caring about anything. This fear was something new. I tried asking a few others for help, but they all acted the same way. They were all scared.

"Finally, I gave up trying to get their help. I banged with my fist at the bronze panels. I thought I heard something like a chuckle from inside, but I must have been mistaken. Then I hammered at the panels with a rock, but nothing happened. I could not get them open.

"I gave up for the time being and went back to the big hall. Everyone there was different now. For two days, the little people avoided me. But finally, things got back to normal. I began to learn what I could of their language. It was actually very simple to learn. There seemed to be few, if any, words about ideas. Sentences were usually no longer than two words. So I decided not to think about the Time Machine and the bronze doors under the sphinx for a while.

"I did some exploring of the area. As far as I could see, the land seemed rich with fruit trees. From every hill I climbed, I could see the palace-like buildings. Then I came upon some round wells. It appeared to me that they must be very deep. Each one was rimmed with bronze and protected from the rain by a little roof.

"I peered down into some of them. I could see no gleam of water. But in all of them I heard a certain sound. It was a *thud— thud—thud*, like the beating of some big engine. A steady, strong current of air went down the wells. I threw a scrap of paper into one. Instead of fluttering slowly down, it was sucked swiftly out of sight.

"I noticed tall towers standing here and there on the hills. Above each one was a flickering in the hazy air, much like you see on a hot day above a beach. Putting things together, I realized that there must be a very big, underground tunnel system. Air must be pumping into the tunnels!

"Other things began to bother me. For example, the big palaces I had seen were just for living. The little people ate and slept there. I could find no machines of any kind. Yet these people wore clothing that must at times need to be replaced. And the little people showed no ability to make anything. There were no workshops or stores. They spent all their time playing, bathing in the river, eating, and sleeping. I could not see how things were kept going.

"Then, again, about the Time Machine:

Something had moved it into the sphinx. *Why?* I could not imagine. I felt I now had some clues about this world, but it was still a mystery. It was as if you had found a stone with words cut into it. Only some of the words were in English. The rest were completely unknown to you. Well, on the third day of my visit, that was how the world of 802,701 seemed to me.

"That day, too, I made a friend—of a sort. A group of little people were wading in a stream. One of them slipped on a rock and began drifting downstream. The main current was swift but not too strong for even an average swimmer. It will give you an idea of how strange these people were when I tell you what happened. No one tried to help her! The poor creature was drowning before their very eyes, but no one seemed to care.

"I waded in at a point lower down. I caught the poor thing and drew her safely to land. She was cold, so I rubbed her hands and feet. By now I had learned not to expect any thanks, so I left her there.

"This happened in the morning. In the

afternoon, I met her as I was coming back from exploring. When she saw me, she smiled and put a big chain of flowers around my neck. Soon, we were sitting and talking. I shouldn't say *talking*. We were mostly smiling and waving our hands. She kissed my hands. I did the same to hers. Then I tried talk and found that her name was Weena. I didn't know what it meant, but somehow it seemed to fit her. It was the beginning of an odd friendship that lasted a week. It ended— as I will tell you!

"Weena was just like a child. She wanted to be with me always. She tried to follow me everywhere.

"It was from her that I learned that fear had not left the world. She was brave enough in the daylight, but she dreaded the dark. I discovered then that these little people gathered into the great houses after dark. Large groups of them slept in the same room. After dark, I never found one of them outdoors, or sleeping alone within doors.

"Yet I missed the lesson of that fear. In spite of Weena's fear, I insisted on sleeping by myself, away from all the others.

"One morning I was awakened about dawn. I had been having strange dreams, and I could not get back to sleep. I got up and went outside to see the sunrise.

"I thought I could see ghosts on the hill. As I looked closer, I did see white figures. Twice I thought I saw a white, apelike shape running quickly up the hill. Once I saw some of them carrying a dark body. I could not see where they went. They seemed to vanish among the bushes. The sun was not quite up, you must understand, so I wasn't really sure of what I saw.

"On the fourth morning, I saw a strange thing. As I was exploring the ruins near the great house, I stopped in shock. From an area of darkness, a pair of red eyes was watching me. Light was reflecting from those eyes, as it does from the eyes of owls and cats. Then I remembered the little people's strange fear of the dark. Was *this* what they were afraid of?

"Overcoming my fear, I reached out and touched something soft. At once the eyes darted to the side. Then something white ran past me. With my heart in my mouth I turned. I saw a strange little apelike figure. Its white hair grew all the way down its back. It held its head down, as if protecting its eyes from the light. I couldn't tell for sure if it ran on all fours or not. Maybe it was only carrying its arms low.

"Holding back my fear, I followed it. It ran into a second heap of ruins. I could not find it at first. After a few moments, I came upon one of those round, well-like openings of which I have told you. This one was half covered by a fallen pillar. A sudden thought came to me. Could the soft white thing have vanished down the shaft?

"I lit a match and looked down. I saw a small, white, moving creature. Its large bright eyes looked at me as it retreated. The sight made me shudder. It was so like a human spider! Now I saw for the first time a number of metal foot and hand rests. They formed a kind of ladder down the shaft. Then my match went out. By the time I lit another, the little monster was gone.

"I don't know how long I stood there. Gradually, the truth dawned on me. Even though the creature I saw didn't *look* human, I know that it was. It appeared that in the future, there were *two* kinds of humans. The little people lived above ground. The white apelike people lived below ground.

"I then figured out why some people lived under the ground, while others lived in the sunshine. It must have started back in our time—in 1895. Back then, many people worked in factories all day. They made the fancy clothes and other luxuries that only rich people could buy. But they spent all their time indoors and hardly ever saw the sun.

"So, in the end, there are the *Haves*, seeking pleasure, comfort, and beauty above ground. Below ground are the *Have-nots*, the workers. No doubt they must pay rent, and not a little of it, to get air into their caverns. If they refused, they would be starved. This is how it seemed to me just then. But I would find out how wrong I was.

"Later, I talked to Weena about what I

had seen. She didn't want to talk about it. She did, however, tell me that the things living below the ground were called Morlocks. She also told me the name of the beautiful little people. They were called the Eloi. She tried to tell me more about the Morlocks. But I didn't know enough of the language to understand what she said.

"I was disgusted with the Eloi. They did nothing to keep things going. The poor Morlocks did all the work. And in return all they got was a terrible life, underground.

"When I asked Weena more questions, she burst into tears. These were the only tears, except for my own, that I ever saw in that Golden Age. When I saw her weep, I stopped thinking about the poor Morlocks. I only thought about how to get Weena to stop crying. It wasn't difficult. Soon she was smiling and clapping her hands. And I was lighting one match after another."

 **Below the Ground**

"It was two days before I could follow up on my new clue. After talking to Weena, I began to feel great disgust for the Morlocks. Their bodies were the half-bleached color of the worms you sometimes see preserved in science labs.

"Then I began to get that restless feeling of one who avoids a duty. I felt that I could get the Time Machine back only if I climbed down one of the wells. You will no doubt understand that I never felt quite safe without someone protecting my back.

"It was this fear, perhaps, that made me continue exploring. I walked for miles in two days. On the second day, I saw a huge building in the distance. It was different from any I had seen up till then. It was deep green, and very shiny in the sunlight. I decided to explore it further the next day.

"But the next morning I realized why I was interested in the Green Palace. It was a way to avoid going down into one of the wells. Getting a grip on myself, I decided to do what I had to do without any further delay. I started out in the early morning toward a well near the ruins.

"Little Weena ran with me. When she saw me lean over the well and look down, she immediately became upset. 'Goodbye, little friend,' I said, kissing her. She watched me start to climb down. Then she gave a pitiful cry. Running at me, she tried to pull me back with her little hands. I shook her off. In another moment, I was in the well. I looked up and smiled to make her feel better. Then, for my own safety, I had to look down at the metal hooks I was holding onto.

"I climbed down about 200 yards as quickly as possible. It was very difficult. The handholds were made for a creature much smaller and lighter than I was. When I stopped to rest at one point, one of the bars suddenly bent under my weight. For a moment I hung on by one hand. After that, I did not dare to rest again.

"As I went lower, the thudding sound of a machine below grew louder. I was very uncomfortable. I thought of trying to go up the shaft again, leaving the Underworld behind. But even as I considered this, I kept climbing down. At last, I saw the opening of a narrow tunnel in which I could lie down and rest. It was not too soon. My arms ached, and my back hurt. I could barely see in the dark, but I could hear the hum of machines pumping air down the shaft.

"I don't know how long I lay there. But at last I felt a soft hand touching my face. I struck a match and saw three stooping white creatures running from the light. Living as they did in such darkness, their eyes were not used to any light at all. So they were not afraid of me in the dark. But the match seemed to scare them.

"I tried to call to them, but their language must have been different from the language of the Eloi. I thought of climbing back out before exploring the tunnels. But I said to myself, 'Stay! You are in for it now.'

"I felt my way along the tunnel, going toward the noise of the machinery. Soon the walls fell away from me, and I came to a large open space. I struck another match and saw that I was in a large cavern.

"Great shapes like huge machines rose out of the darkness. The Morlocks hid in the shadows. The place was very stuffy. The faint smell of freshly shed blood was in the air. I could see a little table of white metal, laid with what seemed to be a meal. The Morlocks, unlike the Eloi, were meat-eaters. I saw part of a leg bone on the table. Even then, I remember wondering what large animal could have provided the meat.

"Just before my match went out, I saw that I had only four matches left. While I stood in the dark, unseen hands began to grab and pull at me. One of them tried to pull my box of matches away. I shouted at the creatures as loudly as I could. They started away, but soon I could feel them coming close again. They pulled at me more boldly, whispering odd sounds to each other.

Then they began to laugh as they came at me. I will confess that I was really scared.

"I struck another match and pulled a scrap of paper from my pocket. The burning paper would last a little longer than a match. At last I was able to reach the narrow tunnel. Then the light went out. I could hear the Morlocks hurrying after me.

"In a moment I was grabbed by several hands. There was no doubt that they were trying to pull me back. I struck another light and waved it in their faces. You cannot imagine how sickening they looked. They had pale, chinless faces. Their pinkish-gray eyes had no lids. But I did not stay very long to look, I promise you.

"I pulled away from the grasping hands and struck my third match. It had almost burned through when I reached the opening to the shaft. Then I felt for the handholds. As I did so, my feet were pulled from behind. I was violently tugged backward. I lit my last match, and it went out right away. But I had my hand on the climbing bars now. I was busy kicking at the Morlocks and was climbing the shaft, while they blinked up at me. One little wretch followed me for some way. As a trophy, he managed to take one of my boots.

"The climb seemed endless. With the last 20 or 30 feet, I felt sick. It was hard to keep my hold. I thought I would faint before I got to the top. But at last, I got free of the well and staggered out into the sunlight. I fell upon my face. Even the soil smelled sweet and clean. I remember Weena kissing my hands, and hearing the voices of other Eloi. Then, for a time, I passed out."

7   A Night Outdoors

"I seemed to be in worse trouble than before. Up until now I was sure that I could escape. I thought my problem was the childish nature of the little people. But now there was a whole new problem in the evil Morlocks. I couldn't help but hate them. Before, I felt as a man might feel who had fallen into a pit. I thought only of the pit and how to get out of it. Now I felt like an animal in a trap, whose deadly enemy would soon come upon him.

"But the greatest enemy I feared might surprise you: *It was the darkness of a night without a moon*. Weena had been talking about the Dark Nights. It was now easy to guess what problems the coming Dark Nights might make for me.

"I felt that I understood this new world

better now. The Eloi might once have been
the rich, and the Morlocks their servants.
But things had changed over time. The Eloi
still had the daylight, of course. The
Morlocks, living underground for so many
generations, had come to find sunlight too
painful to their eyes. The Morlocks still
made the Eloi's clothing and took care of
their needs. But perhaps they continued to
do this only out of habit.

"Ages ago, the Eloi had thrust their
brothers out of the air and the sunshine. Now
those brothers were coming back to them—
changed! The Eloi were being forced to
learn an old lesson all over again. They were
learning about fear.

"Suddenly I thought of the meat I had
seen in the tunnels. I realized that the only
thing it could have been was *Eloi*! It was
clear that, at some time in their past, the
Morlocks' food had run short. Perhaps they
had lived on rats and other vermin. Even
now, man is far less fussy about his food
than he used to be—far less than any
monkey. I tried to look at the thing as a

scientist would. Why should I trouble myself? These Eloi were like fatted cattle, which the Morlocks used as food.

"I would have to find a way to defend myself. I felt I could never sleep again until my bed was made safe from Morlocks. Now I shuddered with horror to think of how many times I had slept outdoors!

"I remembered the Green Palace and decided to go there. I took Weena with me. I had thought it was seven or eight miles away, but it must have been closer to 18. I had brought a second pair of shoes with me, which was good. Since losing one boot to the Morlocks, I had been using them. But the heel of one of my shoes was loose, and a nail was working through the sole.

"Weena ran along beside me. She kept darting off to pick flowers to stick in my pockets. She seemed to think of a pocket as a kind of flower vase. And that reminds me of something else! In changing my jacket I found . . ."

The Time Traveler stopped talking for a moment, and reached his hand into his pocket. Then he placed two dried flowers on the little table and went back to his story.

"By nightfall, the Green Palace was still far in the distance. We came to a thick forest, and I could no longer even see the Green Palace. We were forced to sleep outdoors that night. Weena went to sleep right away. She probably felt safe because I was there.

"I was awake most of the night. I imagine I dozed off at times. But mostly I sat up and thought about this new world. The Eloi had changed over the years, but I still felt I was more like them than the Morlocks. I had to have a plan. First I would find a safe place. Then I would make some weapons. After that, I hoped to find a way to make fire. Nothing, I knew, would be better protection from the Morlocks.

"Finally, I had to find a way to break open the bronze panels under the white sphinx. I thought of a battering ram. My plan was to enter those doors and carry a blaze of light before me. Then I could get in the Time Machine and escape. I would take Weena with me to our own time.

"Finally, the dawn came, pale at first, and then growing pink and warm. No Morlocks had come near us. Indeed, I had seen none on the hill that night. I stood up and found my foot swollen and painful. So I took off my broken shoes and flung them away. Then I woke Weena, and we continued our walk toward the Green Palace."

# 8 The Green Palace

"We got to the Green Palace at about noon. Of course, it was falling apart, just like everything else in this new world. Only little pieces of glass remained in its windows. Big chunks of the building had fallen away.

"The material of the palace turned out to be porcelain. In the front was some writing. I thought that Weena might be able to tell me what it meant. But the idea of writing had never even entered her head.

"The doors were open and broken. Inside, we found a long gallery lit by many side windows. The tiled floor was thick with dust. Then I saw the skeleton of a huge dinosaur in the middle of the hall. *What?* Why, this must be a museum! What other treasures might we discover here?

"At first I was so surprised to find a

museum here that I gave no thought to how it might help me. As I explored, with Weena by my side, I found another short gallery off to the left. This seemed to be devoted to minerals. In another section I found a gallery that seemed entirely devoted to natural history. But everything there had long since turned to dust.

"In one gallery that had no windows, Weena came very close to my side. I saw that the gallery ran down at last into a thick darkness. I could see that there was far less dust here. In fact, it seemed to be broken by a number of small narrow footprints. In the far corners of this gallery I heard an odd pattering and the same peculiar noises I had heard down the well.

"I took Weena's hand, and we left that area at once. We came to a gallery that was full of machines. I knew what some of them were. Others were strange to me. All of them were very old and rusty and falling apart. Then I got an idea. I saw a large machine with a big iron handle on it. I climbed up on it and put all my weight on the handle. It snapped after a minute. Now I had a weapon. It was an iron club, about three feet long!

"With the club in one hand and Weena in the other, I left that gallery. We went into a still larger one. It was full of books that had long since dropped to pieces. Every bit of print was gone. I thought about the great waste of work that had gone into all these books. I must confess that I was thinking mainly about my own writings and what might become of them someday.

"Then we went up a wide staircase. We came to what may have been a gallery of chemistry. I did not think I could find anything useful here. But at one end, this gallery was still well preserved. I looked in every unbroken case. At last, in one really airtight case, I found a box of matches. I tried them. They worked! They were not even damp. I felt better at last. Now I had a real weapon against the creatures we feared.

"Now, I still think it most strange that these matches lasted all those years. But then I found something even stranger. It was a sealed jar full of camphor. I suppose the seal was very tight, for the camphor was still good. I was about to throw it away, but then I remembered that camphor burned well. It would serve, in fact, as an excellent candle. I put the jar in my pocket.

"Now I had an iron club, matches, and camphor. I left that gallery feeling very confident.

"In the next gallery we found a number of weapons. There were guns, pistols, and rifles. Most of them were rusty, though, and there were no bullets. I also found hatchets and swords, and almost took one. But I could carry either my iron club or a sword—not both. I decided that the iron club would be more likely to help me open the panels under the sphinx.

"In another gallery I found two sticks of dynamite. I smashed the case with joy. I lit a stick of dynamite in a little side gallery. I waited 5, 10, 15 minutes for an explosion that never came. Of course the things were fakes, as I should have guessed. It would have been too dangerous to have the real thing in a museum. In a way, I was lucky. If the dynamite had been real, I might have blown up the Time Machine in trying to open the sphinx.

"As night came near, I began to think of our position. I still had to find a hiding place. But that troubled me very little now. Now I had the best weapon against the Morlocks—I had matches! And I had the camphor, too, if a blaze were needed. It seemed that the best thing Weena and I could do was to pass the night outdoors. There we could at least protect ourselves with a fire.

"I thought that in the morning I would surely get back to the Time Machine. I had the iron club, after all. I felt sure that I would be able to open the bronze doors with it."

Fire in the Forest

"We left the Green Palace before the sun set. I wanted to get to the sphinx early the next morning. My plan was to go as far as we could that night. Then we would build a fire and sleep near it.

"As we went along, I started gathering sticks for the fire. Soon I had my arms full. Thus loaded, I moved slower than I had hoped. Weena was tired, and I soon began to feel weary, too. I felt sleep pulling me down, and the Morlocks pulling with it.

"The forest seemed to be about a mile across. I wanted to get through it to the bare hill before we stopped. That seemed like a safer resting place. I thought that my matches and camphor would help us get through the dark forest. But if I were to hold a match in front of us, I would have to stop carrying the firewood. So I put it down.

"Then I thought of setting some of the wood on fire to cover our retreat. Only later would I find out how foolish this was.

"Weena had never seen a fire before. She wanted to run over and play with it. But I stopped her, and we continued through the woods. For a little while, the fire lit the path. Then, looking back, I could see that the blaze had spread to some nearby bushes. I laughed at that, and turned again to the dark trees ahead. The light was very dim, but I could still see well enough to avoid tripping.

"I struck no matches because I had no hand free. I held Weena in one arm, and in my right hand I carried my iron club.

"For some way, I heard nothing but snapping twigs under my feet. Then I seemed to hear a pattering about me. As I pushed on, the pattering grew louder. After that, I heard the same strange sounds and voices that I had heard in the tunnels. Were the Morlocks closing in on us? In another minute or so, I felt a tug at my coat, then something pulling at my arm.

"It was time for a match. But to get one I had to put Weena down. As I searched in my pocket for the matches, a struggle began in the darkness. Weena was silent, but the Morlocks were making strange cooing sounds. Soft little hands were touching my back and neck when I finally lit the match. As I held it up, I saw the white backs of the Morlocks as they ran away.

"I took a lump of camphor from my pocket and got ready to light it. Then I looked at Weena. She was lying on the ground, hardly breathing. I lit the camphor and threw it to the ground. It flared up and drove the Morlocks into the shadows. I knelt down and lifted Weena. Now the woods hummed with the noise of many Morlocks.

"Weena quickly fainted. I put her on my shoulder and rose to push on. Then I had a horrible thought. In the confusion, I had turned myself about. Now I had no idea which way I should be going. For all I knew, I might be facing *toward* the Green Palace!

"I decided to build a fire and make camp where we were. I put Weena down and began

collecting sticks and leaves. Here and there in the darkness, the Morlocks' eyes shone.

"The camphor went out. I lit a match and saw two white forms dash quickly away. I noticed how dry the branches were, for no rain had fallen since I arrived a week ago. Instead of looking for twigs, I began dragging down dry branches. Soon I had a smoky fire, and I could save my camphor. Then I turned to Weena and tried to wake her up. But she lay like one dead. I could not even tell if she was breathing.

"I was very tired. My head was nodding when I again felt the Morlocks touching me. Flinging them off, I felt in my pocket for the matches. They were gone! Now I realized what had happened. My fire must have gone out while I slept!

"I was caught by the neck, by the hair, by the arms, and pulled down. It was horrible to feel those soft creatures on me. I felt little teeth nipping at my neck. But when I rolled over, my hand came upon my iron club. Holding it gave me strength. I started swinging it, and in a moment I was free.

"I knew that both Weena and I were lost. But I wanted to make the Morlocks pay for their meat. I stood with my back to a tree, swinging the iron club before me.

"Then the darkness began to fade. I saw the Morlocks running away from me. In the light, their backs looked not white, but reddish. As I stood there, I smelled burning wood. Looking back, I saw the flames of the burning forest. The fire I had built earlier was now coming after me!

"I looked for Weena, but she was gone.

The fire left me little time to find her. My iron club still in my hand, I followed in the Morlocks' path. It was a close race. Once the flames came near me, but I managed to outrun them. At last I got out of the forest.

"And now I was to see the most weird and horrible thing. The whole area was as bright as day from the light of the fire. On the hill were some 30 or 40 Morlocks, blinded by the light. At first I didn't realize they couldn't see. I struck at them with my bar as they came near me. I killed one and crippled several more. But when I heard their moans, I realized how helpless they were, so I struck no more of them.

"For a while I walked among them, looking for some sign of Weena. But my little friend was gone. It was plain that they had left her poor little body in the forest. In a way, I was glad that she had escaped the awful fate of the other Eloi.

"As I thought of that, I almost wanted to start killing the Morlocks around me. But I controlled myself. From high on the hill, I could now see the Green Palace through the smoke. That helped me get my bearings so I could find the white sphinx.

"So, as the day grew clearer, I tied some grass about my feet. Then I limped toward the hiding place of the Time Machine. My progress was slow, for I was now very tired as well as lame. And I felt terribly sad about the horrible death of little Weena.

"Now, in this familiar old room, it seems more like the sorrow of a dream than a real loss. But that morning, I felt horribly alone. I began to think of this house of mine, of this fireside, of my friends. With these thoughts, I tell you, came a powerful longing that was very painful.

"But just then, as I walked toward the white sphinx, I made a discovery. In my pocket I found a few loose matches! They must have spilled out of the box before it was lost."

§10 The Morlocks' Trap

"About 8:00 or 9:00 in the morning, I came close to Weena's home. For a time I stood on the hill and looked down. Here was the same beautiful scene, the same big palaces and old ruins, the same river. The beautiful people moved here and there among the trees. Some were wading in exactly the place where I had saved Weena. Seeing that spot gave me a keen stab of pain.

"I saw the well-like openings to the Underworld. Now I realized what all the beauty of the Overworld covered. The days of the Eloi were about as pleasant as the days of cattle. Like the cattle, they knew of no enemies. They did nothing to take care of their own needs. And their inescapable end was the same.

"I thought about how this had happened.

Human beings had worked toward comfort and an easy life. It had finally come to a balanced society. The rich became sure of their wealth and comfort. The workers were sure of their life and work. In that perfect world, there had been no problems at all with unemployment and poverty. And a great quiet had followed.

"But the Eloi probably became weak because they had no work to do. The Morlocks at least had the task of keeping the machines going. This is what kept them strong—at least stronger than the Eloi. When other meat failed them, they turned to whatever they could. At least, this is the idea that came to me. I could be wrong.

"After the terrors of the past days, I was very tired. Soon I fell asleep on the little hill. I woke up just before sunset. Now I felt safe from being caught napping by the Morlocks. I walked down the hill toward the white sphinx, carrying my iron club in one hand. My other hand played with the matches in my pocket.

"And then came a big surprise. As I got

near the sphinx, I saw that the panels were open! I hurried over to look inside.

"The Time Machine was there, in the corner! The small levers were still in my pocket. Now I threw my iron club away, almost sorry not to have used it.

"A sudden thought came into my head as I walked inside. For once, it seemed that I understood the Morlocks. Now it was clear that they planned to trap me! I almost laughed at how simple they were.

"I walked through the bronze frame and up to the Time Machine. I saw that it had been oiled and cleaned. As I stood looking at it, the bronze panels suddenly slammed closed. I was in the dark—trapped. Or so the Morlocks thought.

"I could already hear them laughing as they came toward me. Calmly, I tried to strike a match. I had only to put the levers on and then leave like a ghost. But I had overlooked one little thing. The matches were the kind that light only on the box.

"You may well imagine how quickly my confidence vanished. The Morlocks were upon me. In the dark, I made a sweeping blow at them with the levers. Pushing forward, I got halfway into the saddle of the machine, but they kept pulling at me. I had to fight against them to keep hold of my levers. At the same time I had to feel for the place where the levers fitted. They almost got one of the levers away from me!

"But at last the lever was in place. As I pulled it over, the clinging hands slipped away. Then suddenly the darkness fell from my eyes. I found myself in the same gray light I told you about earlier."

 # How the World Ends

"I have already told you of the feeling that comes with time travel. It makes you dizzy—and that is when you're sitting straight up! This time I was not seated well in the saddle. I was sideways and almost falling off. When the machine began to spin, I had to hang on tight. If I fell off, I would be lost. After a while I was finally able to get myself straight on the seat.

"When I was able to see the dials, I was surprised. One dial records single days and another records thousands of days. A different dial records millions of days, and another thousands of millions. Now I saw that the thousands hand was moving as fast as the second hand of a watch. I was blasting into the future!

"But as I drove on, everything changed.

The shifts between day and night grew slower and slower—yet I was still traveling just as fast! The sun stopped setting. Now it just stayed in the west. I also noticed that the moon had vanished, and the earth had stopped spinning.

"I remembered how I had fallen off the machine before. So I was very careful as I slowed the machine down.

"Finally I was able to stop very gently. I sat on the Time Machine, looking around. Now the sky was no longer blue. In the direction of the sun, it was red. Yet everywhere else, it was black.

"I had landed on a beach. From a nearby hill, I heard a harsh scream. I saw a thing like a huge white butterfly go flying across the sky. Then I saw something moving toward me. At first I had thought it was a reddish rock, but now I could see that it was really a huge crab. *Can you imagine a crab as large as this table?*

"As I stared at it, I felt a tickling on my cheek. It felt as if a fly had landed there. I tried to brush it away, but in a moment I felt

it again. When I looked around, I saw another monster crab scuttling up behind me. Its mouth was quivering with appetite. It had been touching me with its feelers!

"In a moment my hand was on the lever, and I placed a month between me and the monster crabs. But I was still on the same beach. Dozens of the disgusting crabs were still crawling here and there.

"I cannot describe the feeling I got in this world. When I moved on 100 years, there was the same red sun. Only now it was a little larger, and a little duller. There was the same dying sea, the same cold air, and the same crowd of huge crabs.

"So I traveled some more, in bursts of a thousand years or more. At last, more than thirty million years from now, the sun took up nearly a tenth of the sky. The crabs had disappeared. The red beach seemed lifeless. Now it was covered with white snow. I felt a chill from the bitter cold. There was ice along the edges of the sea and huge, drifting masses of ice farther out. But most of the ocean was still liquid.

"I looked about to see if any animal life was there. But I saw nothing moving, in earth or sky or sea. Except for the sound of the sea, the earth was silent. *Silent?* It would be hard to describe the stillness of it. All the sounds of people, the bleating of sheep, the hum of insects—all of that was over.

"A horror came over me. Sadly, I set the controls of the Time Machine to the year 1895. Then I pushed the lever."

12 The Time Traveler's Plans

"So I came back. I was so tired that I fell asleep on the machine. The hands spun backward on the dials. When the million dial was at zero, I slowed down. I began to see familiar buildings. Then the old walls of my own lab came round me. Now, very gently, I slowed the machine down even further.

"I saw one thing that seemed odd to me. I think I told you that when I was leaving, my housekeeper was walking across the room—but she seemed to be traveling like a rocket. Now, as I returned, she was walking *backward* across the lab, going out the same door she had entered earlier!

"Finally, I stopped the machine and looked around my old lab. Everything was just as I had left it. I got off the Time Machine slowly and sat down upon my bench. For several minutes, I sat there shaking. Then I became calmer. Around me was my old workshop, just as it had been. I might have been sleeping there all this time—my whole adventure only a dream!

"And yet, not exactly! The machine had started from one corner of the lab. Now it had come to rest in another corner. That gives the exact distance from the lawn to the white sphinx. That is how far the Morlocks had carried my machine.

"Soon I got up and came down the hall. I was limping because my feet still hurt. Looking at the newspaper on the table, I found the date was today. Looking at the clock, I saw it was almost 8:00. And then I heard your voices. Next I smelled the food, and opened the door on you. All of you know the rest: I washed, ate, and then began to tell you the story.

"I know," he said after a minute, "that all this must seem unbelievable to you."

He looked at the doctor. "No, I cannot expect you to believe it. Take it as a lie, then. Say I only dreamed it. Or think of it as a story. But tell me—if you take it as a story, what do you think of it?"

There was silence all around. I looked at the others in the room. The doctor was staring at our host. The editor was looking at the carpet. The reporter looked at his watch. The others were very still.

Then the editor stood up with a sigh. "What a pity it is you're not a writer of stories!"

"What? You don't believe it?"

"Well—"

"I thought not."

The Time Traveler turned to us. "To tell you the truth . . . I hardly believe it myself. And yet . . ."

His eyes then fell on the dried white flowers on the table. He turned his hand over, and I saw that he was looking at some half-healed scars.

The doctor studied the flowers. "Why, I've never seen any flowers like these. May I have them?"

"Certainly not!" said the Time Traveler.

"Where did you *really* get them?" asked

the doctor with a sly smile on his face.

The Time Traveler put his hand to his head. He looked like someone who was trying to keep hold of an idea. "They were put into my pocket by Weena, when I traveled through time." He stared around the room. "Or is it all a dream? Some say that life is a dream, of course. But where did the dream come from? I must look again at that machine—if there *is* one!"

Then he picked up the lamp and carried it down the hall, and we followed him. There in the light of the lamp was the machine, sure enough. It was solid to the touch. I put my hand out and felt it. It had dirty brown spots and smears on the dials. There were bits of grass and moss on the lower parts. One lever was bent a little.

The Time Traveler put the lamp down on the bench. He ran his hand along the bent lever. "It's all right now," he said in a tone of satisfaction. "The story I told you was true, after all." Then he took up the lamp, and we all returned to the other room.

He came to the door with us and helped

the editor with his coat. On the way out, the doctor told him he was suffering from overwork—an idea that made the Time Traveler laugh.

I shared a cab with the editor. He thought the tale was a lie. For my own part, I didn't know what to think. The story was so fantastic, and he told it so well. I lay awake most of the night thinking about it.

I decided to go back the next day and see the Time Traveler again. I was told he was in the lab. But when I went there, I found that the lab was empty. I stared for a minute at the Time Machine. I put out my hand and touched the lever. For some reason the machine started swaying like a branch in the wind. This scared me, so I left right away.

As I walked toward the door, the Time Traveler was just on his way to the lab. He had a small camera under one arm and a bag under the other. He laughed when he saw me and gave me an elbow to shake. "I'm very busy with that thing in there!" he said.

"Tell me the truth—do you *really* travel through time?" I asked.

"Really and truly I do." He looked into my eyes. "I know why you came. Listen, stay for lunch. We'll talk then. Read the magazines over there. If you'll wait half an hour, I'll prove it to you. If you'll forgive my leaving you now?"

I agreed, hardly understanding then what he was saying. He nodded and went on down the hall. When I heard the door of the lab slam, I sat down and took up a daily paper. What was he going to do before lunch? Suddenly I remembered an appointment I had at 2:00. I looked at my watch and saw that I could barely make it. I got up and went down the hall to tell the Time Traveler.

As I took hold of the handle of the door, I heard a click and a thud from inside. A gust of air whirled around me as I opened the door. I heard the sound of breaking glass. The Time Traveler wasn't there. For a minute, I seemed to see a ghostly figure sitting in the spinning shape of the machine. I could see *through* the figure to the drawings on the wall. After rubbing my eyes, I saw that the Time Machine had gone.

I was amazed. How could this strange thing have happened? Just at that moment, the housekeeper came in. "Has he gone out that way?" I asked.

"No, sir. No one has come out this way. I thought I'd find him in here."

Then I understood. I didn't keep my 2:00 appointment. I sat there, waiting for the Time Traveler and the proof he would bring with him. But I am beginning to think that I might have to wait a lifetime. After all, the Time Traveler vanished three years ago.

And, as everybody now knows, he has never returned.

But I can't help wondering. Did he go to the future or to the past? Is he with the cave-dwellers? Did he go back even further—to the age of the dinosaurs? Will he *ever* return?

Or did he go to the future? Maybe this time he went to a better age, one in which today's problems have been solved.

I cannot tell what may happen in the future. I can only live my own life as well as I can. To comfort myself, I often look at the two strange white flowers. They are dried up now, brown and flat. But they remind me that even when mind and strength are gone, love and tenderness still live on in the human heart.